Witch-Training

Training

Flying
Lessons

ROARING GOOD READS

Collins

An imprint of HarperCollinsPublishers

Roaring Good Reads will fire the imagination of all young readers-
from short stories for children just starting to read on their own, to
first chapter books and short novels for the confident readers.

www.roaringgoodreads.co.uk

Other titles in the Witch-in-Training series

Witch-in-Training: Spelling Trouble by *Maeve Friel*
Witch-in-Training: Charming or What? by *Maeve Friel*

Other Roaring Good Reads from Collins

Mister Skip by *Michael Morpurgo*
Daisy May by *Jean Ure*
The Witch's Tears by *Jenny Nimmo*
Spider McDrew by *Alan Durant*
Dazzling Danny by *Jean Ure*

Witch-in-Training

Training

Flying
Lessons

Maeve Friel

Illustrated by Nathan Reed

ROARING GOOD READS

Collins

An imprint of HarperCollins*Publishers*

First published by Collins in 2002
Collins is an imprint of HarperCollins*Publishers* Ltd
77-85 Fulham Palace Road, Hammersmith, London W6 8JB

The HarperCollins website address is www.**fire**and**water**.com

3 5 7 9 8 6 4

Text copyright © Maeve Friel 2002
Illustrations by Nathan Reed

ISBN 0 00 713341 3

The author asserts the moral right to be
identified as the author of the work.

Printed and bound in Great Britain by
Clays Ltd, St Ives plc

Miss Strega's
Hardware Shop
estd. 991

Chapter One

Miss Strega's shop was not like its smart neighbours. For one thing, it didn't have a large plate glass window with eye-catching displays of toys or trainers or books or mobile phones. On wintry afternoons, when bright lights blazed in the other shops along the High Street, Miss Strega's shrank back into the shadows. And if anybody ever popped in to buy some clothes pegs or jam pot covers – and hardly anybody ever did – old Miss Strega bustled out from behind the counter and more or less chased them back out on to the street.

"Just closing up," she would say. "Come back tomorrow."

Children, hurrying home from school, were never tempted to stop and peer in to the shop's shabby, overcrowded window. If they had, they would have seen what a heap of junk it sold; hurricane lamps, mousetraps, bird scarers and flypapers dangled on hooks above a stack of black iron cooking pots and an untidy jumble of balls of twine. Ancient-looking fishing rods and rusty garden forks leant against the door as if they had just been dumped there for the binmen to take away.

So no one noticed when a small broom was propped outside the door on the thirty-first of October. It had a short handle and a bunch of spiky birch twigs tied together at one end. A notice scribbled on a piece of cardboard was tucked into the twigs:

Birch Besom £4.99
Flying Lessons extra

Jessica wouldn't have seen it either, if a sudden gust of wind hadn't snatched her party hat out of her hand. It was a tall, white, pointy hat, the sort that princesses wear, with a long floaty veil stuck on the top.

"Hey," she shouted, "come back." But the hat paid no attention. It galloped along the pavement, skirted around an old lady with a shopping trolley and somersaulted over a baby's buggy. It sailed between the legs of a boy on roller blades, danced over the heads of the shoppers and finally came to land on the spiky twigs of the little broom.

"Flying Lessons extra," Jessica read as she reached for her hat. "How curious." She was just looking up at the peeling old shop sign that hung out from the wall, creaking and groaning in the wind, when a voice said: "Have you come for the broom, my dear?"

Jessica scrunched up her eyes and peered into the shop. She could see a large ginger cat snoozing on top of a pile of books which balanced precariously on the high wooden counter. And behind the counter, in front of

a wall of drawers with shiny
brass handles and little square
labels, there was an old lady,
waving at Jessica to come in. She
was so small, like a little bird with twinkly
eyes, that Jessica could only see her head
and shoulders. She had one hand firmly
cupped over her chin.

"Come in," she said. "I've been expecting
you. I would have closed earlier – Halloween

is always such a busy night for me – but I knew you would appear before long."

Jessica lifted the latch and walked in.

"Now, what can I get for you, my dear? Let me think," said Miss Strega, smiling broadly. "Was it grate polish you were looking for? Or perhaps a new bath plug? Or maybe you need a frying pan?"

Jessica glanced behind Miss Strega at the wall of drawers with their spidery hand-written labels. For a moment in the bad light, the letters seemed to be all mixed up. "Gnats' Spittle, Bats' Legs," she read, "Frogspawn."

She squinted again and the words floated back into place. "Grate Polish, Bath Plugs, Frying Pans."

"No," she said, apologetically. "I don't need anything at all. I just came to get my hat."

"And the broom of course," Miss Strega said. "I left it out especially for you."

"But I... I... don't have any money," Jessica stammered.

Miss Strega shook her head vigorously from side to side. "I wouldn't dream of charging *you*. After all, it is your broom. But you will have to take the lessons of course. They're very important."

Jessica frowned. "*My* broom?"

"Flying is not as easy as it looks, you know," the old lady said, tapping her nose. "Even one lesson can make all the difference."

"Oh dear," thought Jessica, "this is very silly." She backed towards the door. "Thank you very much," she said, "but I don't really need a broom."

"Oh you do," said Miss Strega, "we all do. And don't forget, it's been waiting for you all these years."

"For me?"

"Of course. As soon as Jessica hits double figures, she'll be here, I told it lots and lots of times. And here you are, right on cue, on your tenth birthday!" She clapped her hands and smiled delightedly.

"How did you know that today is my birthday?" Jessica spluttered. "And how did you know my name?"

Miss Strega tapped her nose and smiled even more. Her chin, Jessica could now see, was very, very long. "One of the cats reminded me," she said mysteriously. With that, she came out from behind the counter and steered Jessica back on to the High Street.

"Now here you are," she said, taking the broom and putting it into Jessica's hands. "But do be sensible and come back for the lessons. Beginners often find themselves in sticky situations. One of my girls ended up on top of the Eiffel Tower. It was very, very embarrassing as you can imagine."

Chapter Two

It was getting dark as Jessica walked home. A tiny Batman and a white-sheeted ghost hurried past clutching their bags of Halloween goodies. Large pumpkin lanterns

with jagged mocking teeth grinned at her from windowsills. There seemed to be an amazing number of cats out and about. Big fluffy marmalades, sleek Siamese, silver tabbies and black moggies did figures-of-eight around her legs. They sniffed at her broom and mewed loudly. "Miaou, miaou, miaou," they said. It sounded awfully like "Happy Birthday, Jessica."

At home, Jessica hurried into the kitchen and rummaged about under the sink until she found a roll of large black bin liners. She fetched Sellotape and scissors and paints. Half an hour later, she was standing in front of the long mirror in the hall wearing her new witch's cape and her pointy hat, now painted black with gold stars. She picked up the broom and put one leg either side of it.

"Thank you, Miss Strega," she said to her reflection.

And then, although she was really a very sensible sort of a girl, she opened the front door, pointed the end of the broom at the sky and said, "Vroom, vroom."

Nothing happened.

"I knew it wouldn't work," she said, stepping off and making a funny face at herself

in the mirror. She straightened her hat, stood to attention and seized the broom by its birch bristles. Just for a second, the broom twitched. It bucked forward and then lifted her clean off the ground. Jessica sprang away from it, as if it had given her an electric shock. The broom fell to the ground, shivered for a moment and then lay still.

"HELP!" yelled Jessica, staring at the broom suspiciously. "What happened then? Oh well," she giggled, "at least you didn't carry *me* off to the top of the Eiffel Tower!"

The Halloween party was in full swing when Jessica arrived at the park. There were goblins handing out burgers and hot dogs. The Addams family were running the hot punch stall, as they did every year. A fat frog called Ribbit was setting up an apple-bobbing competition. There were ghosts and headless monsters and Draculas everywhere.

"Attention, attention," announced DJ Frankenstein. "The firework display will start in five minutes."

Jessica moved off with the rest of the crowd to watch. A gorilla was patrolling behind the rope barrier. "Please stand well clear," he growled at the spectators, but everyone ignored him and pressed forward.

Moments later, the fireworks exploded, lighting up the night sky in a dazzling display. Every face was upturned, "oohing" and "aahing" as showers of purple and gold sparks fell back to the earth. Rockets with long tails arced across the sky. Catherine Wheels spun and a stream of silver stars tumbled out of the moon.

Jessica was waving her broom by the handle, spiky end up.

"Look here," said one of the ghosts. "Can you put the broom down? You're spoiling our view."

Jessica sighed. She certainly wasn't going to put her new broom down on the grass where people could trample on it and break it. But just to let the ghost know she was *trying* to help, she bunched the long twigs together in a bundle to make it look smaller.

The next thing she knew, she was propelled backwards at top speed through the crowds, with her feet barely touching the ground.

"Hey," people shouted, "mind where you're going."

"No need to push!"

"Ouch, get off, that's my foot."

Just as Jessica thought she was going to go into orbit, she came to a complete halt and fell over.

"Oops," she said to a luminous green skeleton who kindly helped her up. "Sorry.

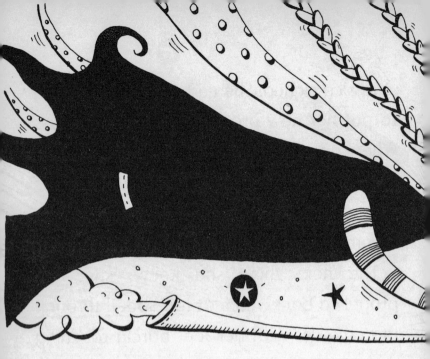

Terribly sorry." And she scuttled off before she could get into any more trouble.

Hiding behind the goblins' burger stall, she peered into the spikes of the broom. She turned it upside down and round and round. She pressed her fingers along the handle and tweaked the twigs. It certainly didn't look as if it could fly. It was just a plain old-fashioned broomstick.

"But," said a voice inside her head that sounded very much like Miss Strega, "flying is not as easy as it looks. Even one lesson can make all the difference."

"That's silly," said Jessica, "brooms can't fly. They can't drag people around the place."

At that moment, the ghost came around the corner with the gorilla. "There she is!" she shouted. "That little witch is a troublemaker."

"Oh dear," muttered Jessica, "I wish I was back home."

The words were hardly out of her mouth when the broom began to buck like a rodeo horse. It took off at a gallop, with Jessica hanging on to the handle. It soared up over the bandstand, over the duck pond and the tennis court.

"Stop!" she yelled, but the broom took no notice. It hurtled on, faster and faster, heading straight for the houses at the top of the hill.

"Help!" she yelled as it skimmed over tree tops and rushed past chimney pots with only inches to spare. "Help!"

At the corner of Jessica's street, the broom stopped sharply. The twigs twitched to the right and left, like a dog listening for a signal. Jessica clung on grimly, hanging motionless above the orange glow of the streetlamp. She closed her eyes.

Then the broom started to move forward again. She could feel it dropping down gently and gliding up the street between the houses like a small plane approaching a runway.

Bump, bump, bump.

Jessica opened her eyes. She had landed on her bottom on the grass in her front garden.

"Bother," she said, and looked at the broom lying beside her. "Flying Lessons are extra."

Chapter Three

"I knew you would be back," said Miss Strega, hastily covering her mouth to hide a giggle, when Jessica appeared at the hardware shop after school the next day.

Jessica turned a little red.

Miss Strega raised an eyebrow. "Did you have any trouble?"

"Well," said Jessica, "I made a wish and…"

"Moonrays and marrowbones!" Miss Strega clapped her hands over her ears and shook her long chin from side to side. "You young witches are always very careless about wishes. Wishes are very powerful, you know."

Jessica stared at Miss Strega open-mouthed.

"What did you call me?" she stammered.

Miss Strega appeared not to have heard her. "Never waste a wish on something you're perfectly capable of doing for yourself. Like flying, for instance. And frankly," she went on briskly, "we should start the first lesson right away. We don't have very much time if you're to be ready for the annual show."

This time, it was Jessica who wasn't listening. The letters on the drawers behind the counter were swimming around. "Grate Polish, Ten-amp Plugs, Ten-inch Nails," Jessica read. "Mmmm. Grate Polish must be Gnats' Spittle. Ten-amp Plugs, perhaps they're Teenage Slugs. And the Ten-inch Nails are Snails' Antennae. It's quite clear really." She gave a little chuckle. "Perhaps I really am a witch!"

"Of course you are," agreed Miss Strega, climbing down off her stool. "Your birthday is at Halloween. Now, let's get started. Flying Lesson Number One. Pop up on your stick, my dear."

Jessica sat astride her broom.

Miss Strega tut-tutted. "There you are, you see. An elementary mistake. You have to sit with the birch twigs in front of you, not behind. Sitting like that is like trying to drive a car with your back to the steering wheel. Unfortunately, it's a common mistake. I blame those pictures in children's books. Now turn it around the other way, then we can start."

Jessica did as she was told.

Miss Strega pointed at the twigs. "These are your controls," she said. "Each one helps you to do different things." She touched the one on the far left. "That's the *Ignition*. Squeeze it very gently."

Jessica gave the twig a little tweak. The broom handle quivered.

"Now the second one, that's *Forward*. Gently, gently, no hurly-burly!" she cried out in alarm as Jessica shot across the floor and collided with a pile of silver tin buckets. "The merest touch is enough when you're indoors. This isn't the fast lane on the Milky Way."

Jessica picked herself up, climbed back on to the broomstick and pressed the twig lightly between her fingers.

"Much better," said Miss Strega approvingly as the broom carried Jessica forward. "Now, the third. That's *Lift*."

Please ring!

As Jessica touched the third
twig, the broom rose gently
and carried her above the high
counter so that her head was almost
touching the ceiling. The ginger cat looked
up at her and winked an orange eye.

31

"You see how perfectly simple it all is," said Miss Strega. "The next twig is *Reverse*. And the very long one beside it is *Pause*."

Jessica reversed slowly towards the wall of drawers and hovered in front of the labels. "Wasps' Stings," she read aloud. "I suppose an ordinary person would think that says Washing Pegs."

"Jessica," Miss Strega said sternly, "that's another day's work. Flying Lessons before Spelling, Brewing and Charming. Now, *Descend*. Tweak the long twig next to *Pause*."

Jessica made a rather bumpy landing beside her teacher.

"Well done for your first attempt. Remember, from the left: *Ignition, Forward, Lift. Reverse, Pause, Descend. Ig-fo-Li. Re-pa-de*."

"Ig-Fo-Li. Re-Pa-De," Jessica chanted back. "And what are all these other long ones for?"

Miss Strega's bony fingers slid over the twig. "*Turn Right, Turn Left, Fast Forward, Fast Reverse.*"

"And these short twigs in the front, are they any use?"

"Of course, my dear, everything under the sun is of use. But don't worry your enchanting little head about them yet. They're for advanced fliers only. Twirling, zooming, spinning, ducking, diving, bucking, moon-vaulting, star-falling. And that one is the *Eject* twig for unwanted hangers-on. Goblins, joy-riding dragons, any sort of pest that tries to hitch a lift."

Jessica looked at her broom admiringly.

"Don't touch any of them, mind," warned Miss Strega. "At least, not until you've got a hang of the basics. I think that's where the girl who ended up on the Eiffel Tower went wrong. Probably hit the *Moon-Vaulting* twig by mistake. And now, allow me to accompany you home. Your mother will be wondering where you are."

Miss Strega fetched her own broom from the cupboard under the stairs and put on her flying helmet.

"That's another thing," she remarked as she fastened the strap under her long

chin. "That hat you have is quite unsuitable for flying, not to mention, awfully old-fashioned. I'll look out something better for you tomorrow."

Jessica followed Miss Strega to the door. On the High Street, they mounted their brooms, tweaked their *Ignition* twigs and sailed up into the twinkly night sky. High above the rooftops, Jessica pressed the *Pause* twig and looked down. The hardware shop was in darkness, a black space between the neon lights of the toy shop and the estate agent's. All over the town, cats padded silently in the long shadows beneath the street lamps as they set off on their secret night adventures, but they all looked up and mewed as Jessica passed over them.

"Don't forget: Flying Lesson Number Two tomorrow," Miss Strega called as Jessica began to descend.

Chapter Four

When Jessica turned up the next afternoon for her second Flying Lesson, she found Miss Strega hovering on her broomstick in front of the wall of drawers. "Winking cats and frisky bats," she said, "I can't find the blinking helmets anywhere. Hop on your broom and give me a hand – remember Ig-Fo-Li..."

Jessica flew up beside Miss Strega and paused. She forwarded and reversed along the rows of drawers, examining the labels. "Sink Plungers, they'll be Lungs of Skunk. Soup Ladles, oh, of course, Pup Saddles." She stopped. "Miss Strega, what on earth are Stencil Hammers?" she asked.

"Well done, Jess. Stencil Hammers are Learners' Helmets. I must admit the spelling leaves a lot to be desired but never mind, just choose one that fits and follow me up to the roof."

Jessica opened the drawer. The helmets were hard on the outside and padded inside, but instead of being round like motorbike helmets, they tapered off into long pointy ends. Jessica found one that fitted and did up her chin-strap before joining Miss Strega on the roof.

The first part of the lesson was practising take-off and landing. Jessica felt as awkward as a swan trying to take off from a lake. She couldn't stop huffing and puffing and her legs beat the air as if she was pedalling an invisible bicycle.

"Keep your back straight, knees together, legs tucked up," Miss Strega repeated endlessly.

"I'll never get the hang of it," Jessica was thinking when suddenly, it all came right.

"Very stylish," Miss Strega declared as Jessica swooped down and made a perfect landing. "You're a born flier. Now, let's take to the air and try something else. Your *Zoom* control is directly below the *Lift* twig. So," she lined herself up beside Jessica, "once again, Ig-Fo-Li and ZOOM."

They rose off the roof together like a pair of silent rockets and zoomed off towards the stars. But they had not gone very far when Miss Strega gasped. "Oh no, here comes trouble."

Hurtling towards them was a gang of goblins, screaming and yelling and shrieking. They flew straight down between Miss Strega and Jessica, cutting them off from one another.

"Oh look, it's a witch-in-training," they jeered, crowding around Jessica. There were so many of them she couldn't fly in any direction. If she steered right, they blocked her. If she veered left, they blocked her.

"Ascend," Miss Strega shouted.

But the goblins flew up like a cloud of locusts and settled on her head and back and shoulders.

"Get off!" Jessica screamed at them, trying to push them off and keep control of the broom at the same time.

Miss Strega zoomed alongside her. "Fast forward, that will shake them off."

Jessica hit her *Fast-Forward* twig and shot off, scattering all the goblins into the dark. Scattering *almost* all the goblins. When she looked over her shoulder, she could see that one of them had managed to cling on to the end of her broomstick and was scrambling back on board.

"Hit the *Eject* twig," shouted Miss Strega, "it's the sh—"

But Jessica, grappling with the goblin who was now clambering over her shoulders, accidentally hit the *Diagonal Lift*. The broomstick flew up and off at a sharp angle, spiralling out of control like a deflating balloon.

"Get off, you," Jessica hissed as she struggled to regain control of the twigs. The goblin, knocked forward by the unexpected diagonal lift, was now lying across the twigs, causing the most tremendous problems. As he shifted position and tried to sit up, he clutched wildly at the controls. The broom lurched to the right, to the left. It ascended and descended. It fast-forwarded and reversed. Miss Strega, shouting directions alongside, was having great difficulty in predicting which way Jessica would move next.

"The *Eject* twig," Miss Strega roared. "It's the shortest one on the b—"

But
Jessica
was already
plummeting out of
the sky, with the goblin
clinging to the *Descend* twig,
laughing hysterically. Jessica looked
down. They were out over the open sea.
It looked very cold and black and wet. She
lurched forward to grab the goblin's scaly

neck and hurl him off, but he was too fast for her. He jumped from the *Descend* control and tweaked a twig that Jessica had never used. The broom suddenly stopped. It began to rotate slowly on its own axis. It built up speed, gradually going faster and faster, until finally Jessica and her pesky joyrider were spinning crazily in the darkness.

"Wey-hey," shrieked the goblin. "Wow."

"You stupid, stupid pest," Jessica screamed back. "Get off my broom."

"Press the *Eject* twig." Miss Strega's voice boomed out in the darkness, though Jessica was spinning so fast she couldn't see where she was. "It's the shortest one on the bo—"

"Of course," Jessica remembered, "the shortest one on the bottom row." She leant forward, dizzily, and let her fingers slide over the bottom row of twigs until she was sure she was touching the shortest. She tweaked and the goblin shot off like a pebble released from a catapult.

"Phew," thought Jessica, grabbing her *Pause* control. She hung motionless in the sky waiting for her head to stop spinning. After a few minutes, she heard the goblin enter the water with a satisfying splash.

"Moonrays and Marrowbones!" exclaimed Miss Strega who had suddenly materialized at her side. "What a lot of hurly-burly that was. Let's go home straight away and make ourselves a stiff brew."

Chapter Five

At the start of Jessica's third lesson, Miss Strega told her about witches' mascots.

"In the olden days," she explained, "almost every witch had a cat, usually a black one, though mine have *always* been ginger. Other witches had owls and some show-offs even had both. Nowadays, our guild, the W3 – that stands for Witches World Wide – are less fussy. They let us choose a mascot for ourselves, unless of course a mascot chooses its witch."

"So, in theory, I could have any animal I like?"

"Jessica, you're wobbling rather a lot," Miss Strega scolded. "Don't lean forward like that. Keep your back straight and your knees together. Tuck your legs up under you. That's better. Now, what was I saying?"

"That I could have any mascot I like."

"Within reason," Miss Strega tapped her nose. "Obviously, having to balance an elephant on the back of a broomstick might be a bit of a nuisance. Not to mention clearing up its you-know-what... Careful, Jessica," she warned, as Jessica, giggling, accidentally hit the *Descend* twig and dropped down into a bank of cloud.

When Miss Strega caught up with her, they flew along in silence for a while. Clouds were very clammy, wet, unpleasant places, Jessica was discovering, not at all as soft and warm and cuddly as they look from the ground. Visibility was bad too. As the clouds got thicker, she could hardly make out Miss Strega's broom ahead of her.

"Let's do a fast-forward climb out of this," Miss Strega shouted back over her shoulder. "I don't know about you, but my cloak is soaked right through. Once we are higher up, it will be quite dry. Ready, Jessica? Come alongside me. *Pause.* That's the girl. Steady. Now, press the *Fast Forward* twig firmly between your right thumb and forefinger and keep your left forefinger on *Lift*. And off we go."

The two broomsticks ascended at speed through the clouds and emerged from their clammy, drippy embrace into a starry night sky.

"This is much better," said Miss Strega, shaking the raindrops off her cape.

"Isn't it very windy?" asked Jessica. "Do you think there might be a storm brewing?"

But Miss Strega wasn't listening.

"Let's see," she said, rubbing her chin. "Lesson Number Three. That's Emergency Stops according to the W3 Rule Book. For the moment, we're going to keep a straight course for the moon, but, when I say STOP, grip the broomstick tightly between your knees and firmly press the *Pause* twig." She looked sternly at Jessica. "I can't emphasize how important the gripping is. Otherwise, you'll launch yourself into outer space without your broom. And then where would we be?"

Jessica looked up at the Milky Way with alarm and down at the ocean of clouds beneath her. She checked the strap of her flying helmet and fast-forwarded to where Miss Strega had paused to wait for her.

"As I was saying," Miss Strega continued as they moved off, "and you can call me picky if you like, but I do think mascots ought to be nocturnal."

"You mean, an animal that likes to be out and about at night-time? Like an owl or a cat."

"Or a frog. Or a bat. Or a fox. There are simply dozens to choose from."

"Mmmm," said Jessica, pensively, "I think I might go for a—"

"STOP!"

Jessica grabbed the *Pause* twig. Her timing with the gripping, however, was not quite good enough and she slid backwards on the broom handle, just stopping herself in time from shooting off into the stars.

"Help!" she yelled, scrambling back along the broomstick. Her knees were knocking together with the fright.

"Carry on, when you're ready, my dear," said Miss Strega calmly, though Jessica could see by the way her shoulders were shaking and her chin was wobbling that she was trying not to laugh.

"Bother," said Jessica, rubbing the back of her knee, "I think I've got a splinter. Nobody

said I'd need kneepads for this flying business." She glared crossly at Miss Strega's back.

Without even turning around, Miss Strega repeated, "Back straight, Jessica. Knees together. Legs tucked up."

Suddenly a large flock of geese was heading towards them. "Gale warning," they honked as they passed by. "Head for home."

Within minutes, black shadows were scudding across the moon. The sky darkened. There was a crash of thunder. Long forked streaks of lightning flashed to the right and left of them.

"We'll have to turn back," Miss Strega shouted into the wind. "Follow me."

The gale grew stronger and stronger. Jessica's broom began to buck all by itself as the wind whipped through the twigs and tossed her hither and thither. Thick damp clouds swirled and churned around her. Storm music welled up. It drummed and clattered and banged.

"Miss Strega," she howled into the darkness, "where are you? I can't see you. Am I going in the right direction?"

There was no reply. Jessica bit her lip. "I suppose I could wish myself out of here," she thought, but remembered Miss Strega telling her never to waste a wish on something she was perfectly capable of doing for herself.

"I expect if I keep flying downwards, I'm bound to hit the ground eventually," she thought again, "even if I land in the wrong country." She sat up straighter on her broomstick, tucked up her legs, firmly gripped the broomstick with one hand to steady herself against the wind and gently squeezed the *Descend* twig with her other hand. As the broom began to drop through the thick wet murk of the clouds, something tickly and fluttery landed near her neck and burrowed under her cloak.

"Oh no," she yelled, "it's that pesky goblin again. That's all I need."

She shook her head and tried to shake it

off, but whatever was there just gripped on more tightly.

"Right," thought Jessica, "you've had it." She leant forward and pressed the *Eject* twig. But the *Eject* twig was obviously out of order for the thing kept fluttering under her cloak. Jessica even thought she heard a little silvery laugh.

"Right," Jessica decided, "I'm not putting up with this."

Gripping her broomstick firmly between her knees, she took the *Descend* and *Zoom* twigs together in her hands. Immediately the broom began to drop out of the sky, falling back to earth like a stone flung from the top of a cliff.

A few minutes later, Jessica crash-landed with a terrific thump outside the hardware shop.

Miss Strega landed beside her and helped her to her feet.

"You know, Jessica, the Zoom-Descend manoeuvre should really only be used if you are landing in water or possibly a lovely soft sand dune," she half scolded her as she led her into the back room of the shop. "It's not meant for pavement touch-downs."

Jessica's head was spinning. She felt so dizzy that she was seeing stars. She seemed to be surrounded by hundreds of Miss Stregas with long pointy chins. Most curious of all, she could hear singing. *Something* or somebody was singing. *Something* or *somebody* was singing *underneath her cloak*.

"What's that singing?" asked Miss Strega. Jessica gingerly undid her cloak. There, sitting on her shoulder, was a small damp brown bird with bedraggled feathers, singing in a very beautiful musical voice.

"What on earth is that?" Jessica asked.

"Well, slap my tummy with a wet fish!" exclaimed Miss Strega. "You have just been adopted by a night-in-gale. That is the best mascot of all. Not only do you get storm protection but you'll have in-flight music too! You lucky, lucky girl."

Chapter Six

Miss Strega was sitting cross-legged on her stool behind the counter, with her chin comfortably cradled in the palm of her hand. "Apprentice fliers..." she read aloud from the

Witches World Wide Rule Book, "must be skilled in twig control, indoor flying, night flying and flying in storm conditions. As part of their training, they should expect to deal with one serious emergency…"

Jessica, who was sitting on the counter patting the cat, looked questioningly at Miss Strega. "You didn't, by any chance, arrange that goblin attack?"

Miss Strega's nose twitched. "So," she carried on brightly, ignoring Jessica's question, "it seems you are ready to move on to Advanced Flying. I'll take you up to the Milky Way tonight."

The Milky Way turned out to be a bright multi-lane inter-galactic highway that cut through the night sky. Jessica could not believe how busy it was.

She constantly had to use her *Ducking* and *Diving* twigs to avoid bumping into all the witches who were whizzing and zooming in every direction. And it wasn't just witches who used the Milky Way. Angels zipped past on their personalized clouds. Red-horned demons sped along on flame-throwing forks. Huge brutes of dragons snorting nasty black puffs of smoke lumbered along illegally in the fast lane, causing long tailbacks. There were gangs of goblins too, but fortunately, they didn't pay any attention to Jessica. They were far too busy racing each other up and down the central reservation with their cosmos-blasters blaring.

As Jessica followed Miss Strega on to a busy junction, she noticed a large banner hanging between two stars:

Strictly no unaccompanied
apprentice fliers
beyond this point
by order BR(EATH) Inc.

"What does that mean – by order BR(EATH)?" Jessica asked Miss Strega.

"BR(EATH) is the W3 flying licence authority. It stands for Broom Riders (Earth And The Heavens)."

Jessica paused. "Do I need a licence?"

"Do keep up, Jessica," Miss Strega called over her shoulder, "there's a minimum speed here on the Milky Way. Of course you need a licence. But the test is not too difficult."

Jessica's jaw dropped. "A flying test?"

"Of course – every witch-in-training has to do a test."

"How many marks do you need to pass?"

"Ten out of ten, of course."

Jessica almost toppled off her broomstick.

"Please tuck up those knees, Jessica," Miss Strega called over her shoulder, "and follow me up into Emergency Air Space. I want to see why the traffic is slowing down. There must be another dragon ahead."

Jessica and Miss Strega hovered above a convoy of magic carpets and peered down the starry highway of the Milky Way. As far as they could see there were no dragons but, for some reason, all fliers were being filtered into a single lane. Further on, the Milky Way Traffic Police had set up a skyway block and traffic had come to a complete standstill behind a flashing notice:

> ### Caution: Phoenix Rising.
> ### Please keep passage clear.

"How infuriating!" huffed Miss Strega. "The phoenix only rises once every five hundred years. It's just our luck that he's doing it on your first night on the Milky Way. This could hold us up for hours."

"What is a Phoenix Rising?" asked Jessica.

"The phoenix is a rather curious old bird," Miss Strega explained. "Only one of them exists at a time. When it dies, it bursts into flames and ascends into space. Then its ashes drop back to earth and it comes alive again. Perhaps we should zoom along to see it. Turn on your emergency tail-lights, Jessica – push that two-prong twig on the second row – and follow me."

Jessica zoomed off after Miss Strega as she soared high into space. The night sky was touched with streaks of red and gold, but as they drew near the skyway block it glowed ever more fiercely. The hot air whirred and hummed and buzzed as if it was alive. Suddenly, the spinning fireball of

the phoenix exploded into view with its feathers blazing, a fiery torpedo aimed at the heavens. At the same time, a young scaly dragon with a load of screaming goblins on its back came galloping down the central reservation and crashed through the skyway block. The watching crowd of genies, dragons, witches, angels and demons gasped in horror. Dragon and phoenix seemed set for a head-on collision.

"Moonrays and marrowbones," yelled Miss Strega. "I'll have to make a spell."

As the fiery ball of the phoenix rocketed upwards and the dragon and his joy-riding goblins bore down on him, Miss Strega began to chant:

"Rise, Phoenix, rise, go on your way
The dragon will stop once I say
'FREEZE!'"

At the word 'freeze', the dragon came to a sudden halt. It dangled in mid-air, shivering a little at the edges like the frame on a paused video.

"Blithering bats' wings!" exclaimed Miss Strega as Jessica and all the Milky Way travellers broke into spontaneous applause. The phoenix fireball continued its upward flight.

"Will you defrost the dragon and the goblins now that the phoenix is safe?" Jessica asked as the traffic began to move forward again.

Miss Strega stroked her chin. "No, I don't think so. They can cool their heels for a year or two. Give them a little time to calm down."

At the next busy T-junction, there was a signpost with two arrows, one pointing left to The Moon, the other pointing right for All Other Directions.

Miss Strega paused and eyed the long queue waiting to turn right.

"Turn left," she announced briskly. "We'll take the shortcut."

Jessica looked up at the round white face of the moon with its mysterious bumps and shadows. Her face dropped. "You mean we're going to do a Moon-Vault?"

"We can go the long way round, if you prefer. I mean, if you're nervous," said Miss Strega.

"I'm not in the least bit nervous," Jessica retorted, firmly tweaking her *Turn Left* twig.

"That's the spirit," said Miss Strega. "It's not at all difficult, just a question of timing and the speed of your approach. You don't want to collide and nudge the moon out of place. Line up here beside me."

Jessica's heart was racing as Miss Strega explained what she had to do. "Hold the *Moon-Vault* twig lightly with your right hand but don't squeeze yet. Zoom forward until you can see Earth and Venus lined up *exactly*, one on your right, one on your left."

As Jessica zoomed, her broomstick strained and bent like a bow. Then as the

lights of Earth and Venus lined up on either side of her, she felt a tremendous thud as if she had hit an invisible launching pad. Her stick began to straighten up.

"Now!" called Miss Strega. "Go for it!"

Jessica squeezed the *Moon-Vault* twig. Then she was off, arching up into space like an arrow. The moon grew huger and huger.

"Oh dear," Jessica prayed, "please don't let me crash."

But the broomstick hurtled on, somersaulted over the curve, only just clearing it, then gathered speed as it plummeted down the dark side of the moon.

"That was BRILLIANT!" Jessica yelled into space as she tumbled towards the familiar blue globe of Earth.

Miss Strega was waiting for her on the roof of the shop. "Congratulations," she said as Jessica dismounted. "By the way, did I mention your flying test is tomorrow?"

Chapter Seven

Jessica was in a flap. She had been flying over the town for ages searching for the Coven Garden Test Centre. Her test was at five o'clock and it was three minutes to five already.

"Miss Strega will be furious if I miss my appointment," she was thinking. "Actually, she'll be furious anyway. I'm never going to pass." She had almost decided to find somewhere to hide for the rest of her life, when she spotted a small roof garden where three old witches, huddled around a large black steaming cauldron.

"That must be Coven Garden," Jessica decided and she zoomed down to the parapet. At the stroke of five o'clock, her name was called out: "Jessica Diamond!"

"Good evening," Jessica said politely, but the three witches ignored her and kept on stirring their brew.

After a very long pause, one of them peered over her half-moon spectacles, winced at the sight of Jessica's torn plastic bin-liner cloak and sucked her teeth.

Coven garden Test centre

"I'm Shar Pintake of BR(EATH)," she said, "the Examiner-Witch, and these are Observer-Witches who will be making sure that no magic spells are used in this test." She sucked her teeth again and fished a piece of paper out of the cauldron. "First of all," she said, "we'd like you to answer a few questions and then we'll move on to the practical flying exercises. Shall we begin?"

Jessica's mouth was so dry she couldn't speak but she nodded. Underneath her cloak, her lucky mascot, now called Berkeley, gave her knee a comforting ruffle.

Shar Pintake cleared her throat. "Very well. At Milky Way junctions, who has the right of way, those already on the Way or those entering?"

That was easy. "The riders on the Way," Jessica answered, "have the right of way at all times except when the phoenix is rising."

"Excellent, now tell us, if you can, the difference between ducking and diving."

"A witch ducks to avoid an obstacle by bobbing and dipping the broom in a sideways direction. Diving is avoiding a crash by leaping and free-falling."

"Mmm," said Shar Pintake. "What is the

braking distance for a broom travelling at two Earth centuries per witch minute?"

Jessica gulped. "Six broomstick lengths?" she suggested uncertainly.

Shar Pintake noisily sucked more air in between her teeth. Her colleagues looked up, quizzically.

"Oh dear," thought Jessica, "that must be the wrong answer."

Next the three witches began to circle their cauldron, chanting:

> *"Broom riders, broom riders,*
> *Hither, thither, they must fly,*
> *Never failing to observe*
> *The ground rules of the sky."*

Then Shar Pintake plunged her hand into the pot and pulled out a pack of cards. "What does this road sign mean?" she barked, holding up a circular sign with a ring of witches.

"That means there's a witches' coven in session at the next roundabout."

"And this?"

"A dragon in a triangle means you should expect slow-moving traffic with heavy loads."

Shar Pintake sniffed. "A cauldron lying on its side?"

"Slippery airspace because of a spilt brew?" Jessica guessed.

The questions came thick and fast with the three examiners taking turns to pull cards from the pack. Jessica's head was spinning as she swivelled to face each of them in turn. If only she had spent more time studying the W3 Rule Book.

"And finally," Shar Pintake said with a loud sigh, "can you identify this hazard?"

Jessica peered at the sign. It was very peculiar. It could have been an old-fashioned pointy witch's hat lying on its side. Or it might have been a jelly bag flying on a pole. Jessica hadn't the faintest idea. She chewed her bottom lip.

"We'll come back to that later," Shar Pintake announced after a long embarrassing silence. "Now go to chimney pot three and we'll start the flying exercises."

Jessica flew off. Things were not going well at all.

"I've failed," she said to Berkeley. "Miss Strega will never forgive me."

Berkeley gave her a cheerful silvery whistle. "Don't give up!" it trilled. "Don't give up!"

Jessica was more confident once she was in the air. She performed a perfect emergency stop. She ducked, dived, zoomed, did an excellent diagonal lift and reversed around the dark side of the moon. It was a faultless performance. She could see that the Observer-Witches were quite impressed. Even Shar Pintake had stopped sucking her teeth.

There was just one tricky moment on the way back to Coven Garden, soon after they had passed Miss Strega who was flitting about on some night errand. Jessica had started her descent towards the landing strip beside the chimney pots when she noticed the sign of the pointy hat and jelly bag. The three witches saw it too.

Shar Pintake did her thing with the teeth. "Has that always been there?" she hissed at the others. Neither had time to answer for a nasty hot little breeze suddenly blew up from nowhere, whipped through their broom twigs and carried all three of them off to one side.

"Ah-ha," thought Jessica, tapping her nose. "It means beware of crosswinds!"

Once Jessica had given the correct answer to the crosswinds' road sign, Shar Pintake asked her to wait a few moments while she and her colleagues had a quiet word.

Jessica sat on the chimney pot stroking Berkeley. The witches seemed to forget all about her. They laughed and cackled and drank some of their brew. Eventually they called her back.

"Jessica," Shar Pintake began with a sniff, "I am pleased to tell you that you have passed your test. You are now entitled to call yourself a Graduate Airborne Spinner and Pilot. Congratulations!"

"I'm a GASP of BR(EATH)." Jessica's face broke into a huge smile. "Cool!"

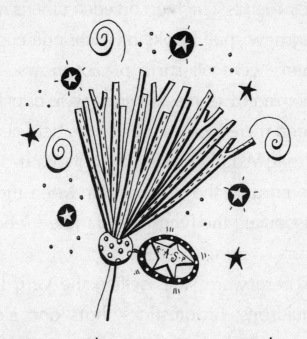

Chapter Eight

The Witches' Annual Air Show was not just about flying displays. It was *the* witchy social event of the year. Witches came flying in from north, south, east and west to meet their friends, catch up on each other's news, buy new spell books or exchange charms. There were all sorts of sideshows – the Zooming Foursome Trick Fliers were astonishing – and there was a mock battle between the Wrong-Way-Ups and the Right-Way-Ups in memory of the Besom War when the W3 introduced the twigs-in-front rule for broom riders.

There were stalls selling the very latest cauldrons, broomsticks, hats and cloaks. Jessica looked wistfully at the cloaks – she was beginning to be quite embarrassed about her shabby bin liner – but she didn't have any money and Miss Strega just wobbled her chin and said, "Moonrays and marrowbones, just look at those prices!"

At the Mascot Rescue Society, Jessica was looking longingly at a jet-black kitten and

two barn owls when there was a sudden outbreak of cheering and clapping outside. A glamorous witch was swooping towards the air show grounds, bobbing dramatically up and down on her broomstick and blowing air kisses to the crowds beneath her. She was tightly surrounded by a retinue of minders and a posse of photographers with all their flashes flashing.

"Hello! Hello everyone!" she cried as she cruised stylishly to a halt, dismounted and threw her cloak over one shoulder. "It's so lovely to be with you all."

"Runny mustard and feather dusters!" Miss Strega exclaimed. "It's one of my old pupils, Heckitty Darling. She's now the most famous actress of all the Witches World Wide. I wonder what she's doing here?"

They soon found out when it was time for the prize-giving ceremony in the BR(EATH) marquee. Shar Pintake began by asking everyone to give a warm round of applause for their distinguished guest. "On behalf of BR(EATH)," she said, sucking her teeth, "I'd like to welcome the legendary Heckitty Darling who has flown all the way from Scotland to present this year's flying trophies."

The crowd went wild, cheering and waving their brooms in the air. Heckitty loved every minute of it. She bowed and laughed and enthusiastically hugged all the winners – including the Best Zoom in a Room and the Synchronized Ducking and Diving Fours. She wiped away a tear as she presented the W3 Bravery Award to a witch who had been cast away alone for three months on a desert island without a working broomstick.

"Finally," she said, "this year only one witch-in-training has successfully completed her Flying Lessons and I am told by the highest authorities in BR(EATH) that she shows enormous promise. They predict a magical and charming future for her – Miss Jessica Diamond, the latest GASP."

As Jessica hovered in front of her, Miss Darling hung the licence plate on the front of

her broomstick. "And now," she appealed to the audience, "let's give our new witch a traditional W3 welcome. Witches arise!"

With that, the whole assembly rose together on their broomsticks. "All hail to Jessica. GASP of the year!" they shouted as one voice.

Jessica, who had now turned a bright

shade of pink, looked down from the stage at the sea of hovering, cheering witches. Miss Strega was in the front row. She was clapping so hard her nose was jerking from side to side, her chin was nodding up and down and she was scattering tears in every direction. Jessica dipped a little curtsey at her.

"Moonrays and marrowbones," Miss Strega mouthed. "What a lot of hurly-burly."

When the cheering had finally died down, Heckitty Darling came to the centre of the stage again. "It's been such fun," she said, "but sadly, my dear friends, I must take to the air immediately."

As the crowds howled and roared their disappointment, Shar Pintake joined Heckitty in the spotlight.

"Ladies, ladies," she called out, "I have a suggestion. Let us all see Heckitty on her

way. Jessica, Miss Strega, will you please escort Miss Darling to the departure runway and we shall all follow."

As Jessica and Miss Strega flew to either side of Heckitty and the audience fell into line behind them, Shar Pintake read out the flight plan. Then the flaps of the marquee were drawn back and the entire world-wide web of witches sailed out into the airy night and up on to the Milky Way, twirling and

spinning, ducking, diving and zooming. At the left turn for Scotland, Heckitty paused to say goodbye. "I wish you the very best," she told Jessica, "and I don't use wishes unwisely. The three of us must meet again."

Miss Strega rubbed her nose and looked quite overcome with emotion.

"Buck up," said Jessica when Miss Darling had whizzed off. "Let's take the short way home, over the moon."

Together, they zoomed forward until they had Earth and Venus lined up *exactly* to the right and left.

"Now!" said Miss Strega stretching out her hand to take Jessica's.

And hand in hand, they vaulted over the moon and came tumbling back down on to Jessica's back garden.

"Now, sleep well tonight, Jess," Miss Strega whispered, "and, don't forget, tomorrow you start your Spelling Lessons!"